So...
and the
Pancake Plot

SOPHIE AND THE ALBINO CAMEL

WINNER OF THE 2006 GLEN DIMPLEX CHILDREN'S BOOK AWARD
SHORTLISTED FOR THE BRANFORD BOASE AWARD
SHORTLISTED FOR THE NORFOLK SHORTS AWARD

'Pure adventure story. An exceptional short novel.' *TES*

'Almost Kiplingesque . . . a wonderful story for readers from 8 to 80.' *School Librarian*

'I like the bit where the snake attacks and Gidaado throws a shirt over its head!'
Leo Taylor, age 6, *Independent on Sunday*

'A joyous adventure story for the 8-10s.'
York Evening Press

'Wonderfully fast moving and humorous style'
Northern Echo

SOPHIE AND THE LOCUST CURSE

'This classy tale is as much a snapshot of West Africa as an adventure, but it has a thrilling camel race and a surprising denouement.' *Daily Telegraph*

'A rich and fascinating insight into West African culture.'
Carousel

Sophie and the Pancake Plot

STEPHEN DAVIES

ILLUSTRATED BY DAVE SHELTON

ANDERSEN PRESS
LONDON

First published in 2008 by
Andersen Press Limited,
20 Vauxhall Bridge Road, London SWIV 2SA
www.andersenpress.co.uk

British Library Cataloguing in Publication Data available

ISBN 978 1 84270 795 1

Typeset by FiSH Books, Enfield, Middx.
Printed and bound in Great Britain by
CPI Bookmarque Ltd, Croydon, CR0 4TD

For Joshua and Milly

Chapter 1

Hundreds of horns gleamed in the African sun. Hundreds of tails flicked to and fro. Hundreds of hooves trudged through narrow streets. This was rush hour and Sophie Brown was being jostled along in a crowd of cows which were heading out of Gorom-Gorom to graze. The animals moved in one great mass, eyes fixed on the ground – like Londoners on their way to work, thought Sophie. Even after three years living in

1

Africa, she still couldn't help thinking about England. Most of her friends were back there, after all.

Except for Gidaado the Fourth of course. He lived here in Gorom-Gorom and was Sophie's best friend by far. Gidaado didn't know when his birthday was but he looked about ten, which was the same as her. He knew hundreds of songs and jokes and he had a very cool albino camel called Chobbal. What more could you want in a friend?

Sophie put her hand over her mouth to protect herself from the clouds of dust being kicked up by the commuting cows. She screwed up her eyes and squinted at the mud-brick houses to her left and right, trying to remember where Madame Maasa's place was. This morning Sophie was on a very special errand for Gidaado – he had given her a pocketful of money and told her to buy three thousand pancakes.

There was the house! And there was Madame Maasa, sitting outside on a small wooden stool. She was hunched over her frying pan and gazing into it intently, like a fortune-teller over a crystal ball. Sophie elbowed her way through the herd of cows and entered Madame Maasa's yard.

'Hello,' said Sophie. 'Did you pass the night in peace?'

'Peace only,' said Madame Maasa. She did not even look up from her frying pan.

'How much are your *maasa*?' asked Sophie.

'Ten francs each.'

Sophie looked at the pan. *Maasa* were small African pancakes – blobs of batter fried in vegetable oil. They smelled delicious.

'What if I buy a hundred?'

Madame Maasa flipped a pancake with her spatula. 'In that case,' she said, 'five francs each.'

'What if I buy three thousand?'

Madame Maasa shrieked with laughter in mid-flip, causing one of her pancakes to sail through the air and flop down in the dust at Sophie's feet, where a chicken began pecking at it. 'If you buy three thousand *maasa*,' chuckled Madame Maasa, 'you can have them at three

3

francs each, and I'll even give you this stool I'm sitting on.'

'Deal,' said Sophie.

'What?'

Sophie held out a green banknote. 'Here's five thousand francs. I'll give you the rest when you've finished.'

Madame Maasa spluttered. 'But...but ... you can't...I can't...'

'I'll pick up the first thousand tonight,' said Sophie.

'But—'

'I've got to go,' called Sophie, breaking into a run. 'Peace be with you!'

Madame Maasa scowled and hit the chicken on the head with her spatula. Three thousand pancakes! What could this addle-brained white girl want with three thousand pancakes? Still, she thought, it was a good deal. Nine thousand francs could buy a lot in this town.

Sophie's next stop was the marketplace. Today was market day and the town was full of buying, selling, gossiping people. Muusa ag

Bistro was pacing the streets selling extra-long turbans. Baa Jibi Norme was shouting for people to come and buy his cheap designer sunglasses. Salif dan Bari was in his usual spot, selling New Salif Extra-Plus Anti-Snakebite Pills. And in the middle of it all was Gidaado the Fourth. He was standing – yes, *standing* – on the snowy hump of his albino camel, and an eager crowd was gazing up at him.

'There are two types of people in this world,' Gidaado was saying. 'Firstly, there are those who love General Alai Crêpe-Sombo.'

'THAT'S US!' shouted a voice in the crowd.

'And secondly—' Gidaado paused.

'Yes?' cried the crowd.

'Secondly—'

'YES?'

'Secondly, there are those who ARE General Alai Crêpe-Sombo!!!'

The crowd fell about laughing.

'The second group has only one member!' shouted Gidaado and the front row of the audience began to cheer.

Gidaado must be loving this, thought Sophie. *He always did like being the centre of attention.*

Gidaado the Fourth was a griot, which meant that he spent all his time telling stories and singing the praises of Very Important People. These days he was working for General Alai Crêpe-Sombo, helping to drum up support for his election campaign. The election of a new president was only three days away.

'Give me a Crêpe!' shouted Gidaado.

'CRÊPE!' yelled the crowd.

'Give me a Sombo!'

'SOMBO!'

'Give me a Bombo-Combo-Wombo-Zombo-Thombo-Crêpity-Sombo!'

'BOMBO-COMBO-WOMBO-ZOMBO-THAhahahahaha . . .'

'Who do you want for president?'

'CRÊPE-SOMBO!!!'

'Time for a song!' shouted Gidaado. 'Somebody please pass me my *hoddu*.'

The crowd stamped and cheered. Gidaado reached down to take hold of his three-string guitar, then stood and began to pluck the strings. Sophie grinned and squeezed in amongst the spectators.

'Actually,' said Gidaado, 'I don't think I should. This song might give you nightmares.'

'Sing it!' cried the crowd.

'I really don't know.'

'SING IT!'

'All right. Don't say I didn't warn you.' Gidaado the Fourth, official praise singer for General Alai Crêpe-Sombo, swelled and began to sing in a high-pitched voice:

'One night Alai Crêpe-Sombo was a-
      shepherding his sheep
Along a moonless footpath in the Scary
      Fairy Wood.
Two hundred scary fairies were awoken
      from their sleep,
And they sneakily surrounded him as scary
      fairies do.'

The crowd had gone from mad excitement to

deathly silence. Sophie knew what the scary
fairies were; they were forest djinns which lived
in trees and came out at night to cause trouble.
People in Gorom-Gorom were terrified of them.

"'Who's there?" said General Sombo and his
voice was loud and deep.
"Are you friend or are you foe or are you
something in-between?"
"We're foe," said Scary Fairy One. "We're
gonna eat your sheep,
And if you try and stop us we will also eat
your spleen."

"Eeew," said General Sombo and he gave a
gallant laugh.
"That sounds to me a thoroughly unappe-
tizing feast.
Your hunger might just vanish when you're
splatted with my staff.
You lily-livered fairies do not scare me in the
least."

What followed was as bloody as the Fall of
  Timbuktu,
As heroic as the capture of the Koupiela
  Keep.
Crêpe-Sombo gave those wicked djinns a
  lesson in Kung Fu,
He de-fairy-fied the forest and defended all
  his sheep!'

Gidaado's audience breathed a sigh of relief
and began to clap. The song had pushed all the
right buttons – fear of the dark, fear of djinns
and love of sheep. Crêpe-Sombo was a hero.

Sophie joined in the clapping but something
seemed not quite right. After all, General Crêpe-
Sombo was a soldier, not a shepherd. She
nudged the girl next to her.

'What do you think?' Sophie whispered.
'Truth or legend?'

'Truth, of course,' said the girl. 'You think the
General would think twice about beating up a
few djinns? Look at him. You can see his
muscles rippling even under his uniform.'

9

It was true, General Alai Crêpe-Sombo was a fine figure of a man. There he stood, more than six feet tall and built like a comic-book hero. The rows of medals on his barrel-like chest gleamed in the midday sun. As Sophie watched, the General crouched slightly and bunched his fists, then sprang onto the bonnet of his Land Rover and up onto the roof rack. The crowd went wild. Ground to roof rack in two leaps: quite a feat.

A small bearded man wearing a red beret clambered up onto the roof of the Land Rover and stood beside General Crêpe-Sombo. Sophie recognised him as Furki Baa Turki, the loudest town crier in the entire province.

'*Hommes de Gorom-Gorom!*' cried General Crêpe-Sombo in French, shielding his eyes from the sun. 'Men of Gorom-Gorom, I stand here today and I am filled with compassion. I see you bumbling along, bleating to each other, Which way, which way, which way should we go? Men of Gorom-Gorom, you are sheep without a shepherd!'

Furki Baa Turki translated the General's words into Fulfulde. His voice was so loud that Sophie had to put her fingers in her ears.

'He's so right,' murmured the girl next to her.

'Men of Gorom-Gorom,' roared the General, 'let Crêpe-Sombo be your shepherd!'

'LET CRÊPE-SOMBO BE YOUR SHEPHERD!' yelled Furki Baa Turki, and the crowd nodded.

'Men of Gorom-Gorom,' roared the General, 'follow Crêpe-Sombo!'

'FOLLOW CRÊPE-SOMBO!' yelled Furki Baa Turki, and the crowd beamed.

'Men of Gorom-Gorom,' roared the General, 'vote for Crêpe-Sombo!'

'VOTE FOR CRÊPE-SOMBO!' yelled Furki Baa Turki, and the crowd applauded.

'Women of Gorom-Gorom,' roared the General, 'that goes for you too!'

'WOMEN TOO!' yelled Furki Baa Turki.

Sophie turned and pushed her way through the crowd. Interesting though it was to watch Gidaado the Fourth and Furki Baa Turki, she

11

had more important things to do. She hurried around the various market stalls, buying batteries for her radio, goat meat for her dad and cucumbers for her tortoise.

'Did you remember to order the General's pancakes?'

The voice at Sophie's shoulder made her jump. It was Gidaado.

'Of course I remembered,' said Sophie. 'Three thousand pancakes coming right up.'

'Good.' Gidaado seemed relieved. 'What do you think of the rally?'

Sophie curled her lip. 'Women of Gorom-Gorom, that goes for you as well,' she mimicked. 'I don't like your boss's attitude.'

'You have no taste,' said Gidaado. 'Personally, I think he is magnificent.'

'He pays you to think that,' said Sophie. 'What was all that "One night Alai Crêpe-Sombo was a-shepherding his sheep" stuff?'

Gidaado grinned. 'That was my idea,' he said. 'It makes the herders love him. It makes them think he's one of them.'

'So it's not true.'

'Not strictly, no. It's an epic poem. It's a praise song. It's a part of our tradition.'

'It's a pack of lies,' said Sophie.

Gidaado grinned. 'You know nothing,' he said. 'See you later.'

Chapter 2

The full moon cast eerie shadows across Gorom-Gorom's marketplace. Usually the market was empty at night, but tonight there was a large crowd, all dressed up in their Friday best. Furki Baa Turki and the other town criers had done their job well that afternoon, marching up and down the alleyways of the town, banging their tam-tam drums and announcing the Great Pancake Giveaway. They had even announced it on *Start the Day with Ali Cisse*, the wake-up show on Gorom-Gorom's new FM radio station.

Madame Maasa had done her job well, too. She had fried the first batch of one thousand *maasa* and heaped them onto four enormous plates. When Sophie came to collect, the pancake woman was all smiles.

'I heard the criers!' said Madame Maasa. 'To think that I have fried a thousand *maasa* for General Crêpe-Sombo, and that tomorrow I get to fry a thousand more. What an honour! Why didn't you tell me they were for him?'

Sophie lifted the first plate onto her head and gripped it tightly with both hands. Madame Maasa's three daughters came and took the other three plates, balancing them lightly on their heads and moving off towards the marketplace.

'Straighten your back, Sophie,' said Ramata, the eldest of the three. 'Your *maasa* are going to fall off.'

'Look straight ahead of you,' said Haibata.

'Don't bob up and down so much,' said Amnata.

'Have a good time,' yelled Madame Maasa. 'Don't forget to bring my plates back!'

The Crêpe-Sombo Campaign Land Rover was parked on the edge of the marketplace. It was black and had dark bulletproof windows.

Sophie knocked on the back door of the Land Rover with her knee and it swung open. Inside, by the dim orange light of a paraffin lamp, two men were slicing bananas. One of them wore an army uniform and had a long scar running from the corner of his left eye down to his chin. The other was a giant of a man whom Sophie recognised as Pougini, General Crêpe-Sombo's bodyguard.

'Where's Crêpe-Sombo?' asked Sophie.

'That's *General* Crêpe-Sombo to you,' said the soldier. 'You're late.'

Sophie and the girls put down their plates and began to fold slices of banana into the pancakes. With all of them working together it did not take long.

A sudden snort directly behind Sophie made her jump, and she turned round to see a large pair of nostrils flaring in her face. Above them a pair of liquid eyes gleamed in the moonlight. The eyelashes were very long.

'Listen, Chobbal,' said Sophie. 'If you think you're getting any of these pancakes, think again.'

Chobbal was the Fulfulde word for spicy millet porridge. It was also the name of Gidaado's albino camel.

'*Salam alaykum*, Sophie.' Gidaado was perched on Chobbal's hump, grinning in the moonlight. 'Are we ready to go?'

'Yes,' said Sophie, 'but I want you to know that I'm only doing this because you and me are friends, not because I want Crêpe-Sombo to win.'

'Whatever.' Gidaado rode off a short distance, stood up in the saddle and began to sing at the top of his voice.

'The delightful General Crêpe-Sombo
Has a dish of Election Delights.
There's a sugary treat for each voter to eat.

Get your crêpe from Crêpe-Sombo tonight!'

A ripple of excitement ran through the crowd. The moonlight and song and the promise of food were making them giddy with pleasure. On and on Gidaado sang:

'When Crêpe-Sombo comes into power
He will rename this market Crêpe Plaza;
The history books will honour the cooks
Who pan-fried his Victory *Maasa*.'

Sophie passed a plate of banana pancakes up to Gidaado and he began to throw them into the crowd. Eager hands reached out to catch the delicious morsels as they rained down.

'Crêpe-Sombo's a generous giver,
Crêpe-Sombo's the Lord of largesse,
Believe all the hype, he's the head-of-state type,
Have a pancake on General C.S.'

The people of Gorom-Gorom laughed and munched and told each other what a good fellow General Crêpe-Sombo was. It took a very big-hearted man to distribute crêpes on such a large scale. He would surely make a fantastic president.

Gidaado held up the last pancake, swung his arm round and round and then lobbed it high into the air. All eyes were on the pancake as it flipped over and over in the moonlight, and then – BANG!

A shower of tiny stars filled the sky. For many of the people in the crowd, this was the first time they had seen a firework. Children shrieked. Herders ducked and cowered. Women grabbed hold of each other and hid their faces under their shawls. Young men whipped their staffs off their shoulders and brandished them, alert and battle-ready.

Another firework fizzed through the air and exploded into a frenzy of coloured sparks. Gorom-Gorom was not under attack. This was all part of the Crêpe-Sombo Spectacle.

And there he was! The General was standing on the roof of Salif dan Bari's snake-pill shop, silhouetted against the backdrop of coloured stars. His feet were planted wide apart and he held a writhing snake in each hand. Gidaado was right, thought Sophie – Crêpe-Sombo is magnificent. God-like, even.

'*Hommes de Gorom-Gorom*,' thundered Crêpe-Sombo in French. 'We are at war!'

Furki Baa Turki translated the General's words into Fulfulde and a gasp of horror rose from the crowd.

'We are at war with the sand!' cried Crêpe-Sombo. 'Every year the great Sahara Desert moves further and further south. Soon it will sweep over us all!'

Sophie glanced back over her shoulder, half-expecting to see a wall of sand careering towards her like a tsunami wave.

'Ten years from now,' said Crêpe-Sombo, 'your homeland will be a distant memory. Gorom-Gorom, Yengerento, Bidi, Menegu, Giriiji – all these precious villages will be buried underneath the dunes. You do not have much time!'

Time! Sophie looked at her watch and saw that it was already half past eleven. If she stayed out any longer her father would go mad with worry.

'This is a war you must not lose,' continued Crêpe-Sombo. 'You will need a Commander-in-Chief who does not know the MEANING of the word "lose"!'

Sophie slipped away from the crowd and hurried back to the Land Rover. She would have to pick up Madame Maasa's empty pancake plates and then run straight home. Dad often worked late, and if she was really lucky, he would not have noticed that she was gone.

As Sophie reached out to open the back door of the Land Rover, she heard voices inside. She stopped and listened.

'The crowd loves him,' said the first voice. 'When he pauses for breath, they go so quiet you could hear a skink sneeze!'

'They'll vote for him now,' replied the other,

'but the question is, will they fight for him when he declares war?'

When he declares war? Sophie frowned. *What on earth are they talking about?*

Sophie opened the door. Pougini and the soldier were sitting inside eating pancakes. They jumped when they saw her.

'What war?' said Sophie sweetly.

The men looked at each other. Pougini's eyes flashed angrily in the lamp light.

'*You*,' he said, and he managed to inject that one word with fierce dislike and menace.

'Hello, Pougini,' said Sophie. 'I thought bodyguards were supposed to bodyguard?'

'I'm taking a break.'

'You're eating pancakes.'

'So?'

'I heard one of you say something about a war,' said Sophie. 'What war might that be?'

The soldier clicked his tongue angrily. 'You were obviously not listening to the General's speech,' he said. 'The General is declaring war on sand. The people of the north must fight.'

'They must plant trees,' said Pougini. 'Thousands and thousands of trees.'

'Trees are good,' said the soldier. 'They act as a barrier against the advance of the sand.'

The two men nodded at Sophie like oversized monitor lizards, and then suddenly Pougini remembered his anger. 'What do you want anyway?' he snapped.

'Madame Maasa's plates. She needs them for tomorrow's pancakes.'

'Here.' The bodyguard thrust the pile of plates roughly into Sophie's hands. 'In future, don't creep up on people.'

'Sorry,' said Sophie.

Chapter 3

It was past midnight when Sophie arrived home. She spat on the hinge of the main gate and it swung open silently. She was in luck: the light in her dad's study was on, which meant that he was still hard at work.

After the death of Sophie's mother four years ago, Sophie and her dad had come to Africa to start a new life. Dad was a botany professor and he busied himself with researching the plant life on the edge of the Sahara Desert. His special interest was carnivorous plants. Two years ago he had amazed the scientific world with his discovery of the desert flytrap *Drosophyllum Brownum*, and he still passed most of his time in his study doing experiments on it.

Sophie crossed the yard and slipped in through the front door. She was tiptoeing towards her bedroom when suddenly the door of the study opened and out walked her dad. He seemed surprised to see her.

'What's the matter, love?' he said. 'Can't you sleep?'

Sophie breathed a sigh of relief, tinged with sadness. Dad had not even noticed her absence.

'It's a warm night,' she replied, which it was.

'In that case,' said her father, 'I have just the thing for you.'

Sophie followed her father into the study. It was dark inside and smelled faintly of compost.

'Isn't she beautiful?' said her dad, twisting the neck of his desk lamp so that it shone on the desert flytrap.

Sophie had seen the plant dozens of times but she was indeed a beauty. Long slender leaves uncoiled from a central rosette and there were six or seven bright yellow flowers.

'Look,' said Sophie's father, pointing. On one of the flytrap's leaves there was a black speck surrounded by a red smudge.

Sophie stared. 'Is that—?'

'Blood?' Sophie's father nodded. 'As a matter of fact, it's *my* blood. A mosquito bit me and now Phyllis is eating him.'

Phyllis was Mr Brown's affectionate nickname for the *Drosophyllum Brownum*.

'She produces a delicious aroma which only insects can smell,' continued Sophie's dad. 'The insect lands on a leaf and gets stuck. The more it struggles, the stucker it gets, and finally it suffocates and dies.'

'And then Phyllis eats it,' said Sophie. 'You've already told me.' She was about to add 'hundreds of times' but stopped herself just in time. Dad loved talking about his flytrap and she didn't want to hurt his feelings.

'I know,' said Dad, wagging his finger, 'but this is Phyllis's first mosquito. Just think of that, Sophie: *a plant which eats mosquitoes*. With enough of these beauties we could wipe out all the diseases spread by mosquitoes – maybe even malaria itself!'

Sophie stifled a yawn. 'You said you had something for me?'

'Oh yes.' Dad snapped off one of Phyllis's yellow flowers and held it out for Sophie. 'Eat this,' he said.

Sophie took the flower and stared at her father as if he had gone out of his mind.

'Go on,' said Dad. 'You said you couldn't sleep. This is the perfect cure for insomnia. You'll be asleep in twenty-five seconds.'

'Twenty-five seconds?' said Sophie. 'How do you know?'

Her dad fidgeted with his sleeve and said nothing.

'Dad!' Sophie put her hands on her hips like her mum used to do. 'How many times have I told you *not to eat flowers*? It could be dangerous.'

'I did it for Science,' mumbled her father. 'Anyway, it's here if you want it.'

'Well, I don't,' said Sophie. 'I'd rather count sheep.' She turned on her heel and stomped out of the room.

A minute later she was back. 'I forgot to say good night,' she said.

'Did you?'

'Yes.'

'Oh,' said Dad. 'Good night.'

'Good night,' said Sophie.

An hour later, Sophie was half wishing she had eaten the flower. What kept her awake was not the heat but rather the thoughts going round and round in her head. She saw Crêpe-Sombo waving his snakes against a backdrop of falling stars. She saw Gidaado balancing on Chobbal's saddle, singing his heart out in praise of his boss. She saw the soldier and the bodyguard scowling in the dim light of a paraffin lamp. And over and over she heard that voice: *The question is, will they fight for him when he declares war?*

According to Crêpe-Sombo's men, the coming war was to be fought against the invading sand. But Sophie was not satisfied by that explanation. *Will the people fight for him when he declares war?* This was not tree-planting talk. This was about real war – real, terrifying war.

As Sophie slid into fretful sleep, she pictured an enormous desert flytrap waving its tentacles beguilingly at a crowd of tiny people. Its sweet aroma and beautiful yellow flowers made it extremely attractive to those who milled around it – right up until they became locked in its deadly embrace.

The alarm clock went off at half past six in the morning. Sophie groaned. Four hours of sleep was not enough for any human being, but she had no choice about getting up. Discipline was enforced harshly at Gorom-Gorom Elementary School, and Sophie's class teacher Monsieur Lapin had been known to beat latecomers with a *gurmoohi* branch.

In four minutes flat Sophie got up, dressed, brushed her teeth, bolted down a bowl of maize flakes and dashed out of the door. She crossed the yard, swung open the gate and ran smack into a pair of fine strong teeth. Camel teeth.

'*Salam alaykum*, Sophie,' said Gidaado the Fourth, looking down at her from Chobbal's saddle. 'Come with me.'

'I can't,' said Sophie. 'Today is a school day. It's fine for you to spend all your time singing and dancing and mucking about, but some of us have to study.'

'You don't understand,' said Gidaado. 'General Crêpe-Sombo is asking for you. He wants you to translate on Gorom Radio this morning.'

'What about Furki Baa Turki?' said Sophie. 'Why can't he do it?'

'Furki Baa Turki is in bed with a sore throat. He can hardly speak at all.'

'I'm very sorry about that,' said Sophie, 'but you'll have to find someone else. It's already five to seven and I should be in school.'

31

Gidaado's face fell. 'There isn't time to find anyone else. It's you or no one. Please, Sophie, I really need you to do this for me.'

Sophie sighed and clambered up into the saddle behind Gidaado. Playing truant was a serious offence and Monsieur Lapin would be furious when he found out. But Gidaado was her only friend in Gorom-Gorom and he needed her help.

'Hoosh-ka!' cried Gidaado, and Chobbal began to trot in the direction of the radio station, which was way out of town on the Yengerento road.

'Gidaado,' said Sophie. 'Who's that soldier with the scar who is always hanging around General Crêpe-Sombo?'

'That's not just any old soldier,' said Gidaado. 'That's the chief of the army brigade here in Gorom-Gorom. His name is Lieutenant Yameogo.'

'I see. So they're friends, are they?'

'Must be.'

Gidaado looked anxiously at the sun. 'What's the time, Sophie?'

'Three minutes to seven.'

'*Zorki*,' said Gidaado. 'In that case, we should probably – HOOSH-BARAKAAAAA!!!'

Chobbal flattened his ears and broke into a gallop. Globs of camel saliva spattered the children's faces and clouds of sand and dust flew up behind them.

'GIDAADO!' shrieked Sophie, grabbing him round the waist so as not to fall off. 'What's the rush? When does your radio programme start?'

'Seven o'clock! The General told me that if I'm late he will do to me what he did to the scary fairies.'

'I thought you made up that story yourself.'

'I did,' said Gidaado, 'but it's better not to take the risk, don't you think?'

Chapter 4

Thanks to Chobbal, they were only two minutes late. They found General Crêpe-Sombo's Land Rover parked outside the radio station, and Sophie noticed the bodyguard Pougini sitting in the driving seat.

Crêpe-Sombo himself was already in the studio. He was sitting on a swivel chair swigging a glass of strong black coffee. He glared at the children as they came in.

'There is only one thing worse than being late,' said General Crêpe-Sombo.

'What's that?' said Sophie.

'Running away from a battle,' said the General.

Worse than that is starting *a battle*, thought Sophie, but she bit her lip and kept quiet.

Ali Cisse, the radio presenter, grinned at them from the other side of a soundproof window and held up two fingers. Two minutes till showtime. Gidaado took out his *hoddu* and began to tune it quietly. He was so nervous his teeth were chattering. He had never sung on the radio before.

General Crêpe-Sombo adjusted the microphone in front of him, then glanced at Gidaado and scowled. 'Tell the griot to make his teeth be quiet,' he said to Sophie, 'if he wants to be paid this week.'

'What did he say?' asked Gidaado, who did not understand French.

'He said don't be nervous,' whispered Sophie in Fulfulde. 'He said you're a star and you'll be absolutely fine.' Gidaado grinned and his teeth stopped chattering.

Crêpe-Sombo looked at Sophie. 'I've forgotten your name,' he said.

'Sophie Brown,' said Sophie.

'I know what you are thinking, Sophie Brown,' said the General. 'You are thinking how lucky you are to be chosen as my translator for today. You are thinking how proud your mother will be when she hears your voice on Gorom Radio.'

'As a matter of fact,' said Sophie, 'my mother is—'

'I have a daughter myself, of course,' interrupted the General. 'Marie has just started at boarding school in Paris. That's in France, that is.'

Suddenly a red light came on in the studio and Ali Cisse put his finger to his lips. Any second now they would be live on air.

'*SALAAAAM ALAAAAAAYKUM*, GOROM-GOROM!' said Ali Cisse. 'You're listening to Gorom Radio 98.8 FM, and this is *Start the Day with Ali Cisse*. The song I just played was *Things Can Always Get Worse* by Bandé Zacharie. Now, I have a special guest with me in the studio this morning: Presidential Candidate General Alai Crêpe-Sombo! *Salam alaykum*, General.'

'*Alaykum asalam*,' replied Crêpe-Sombo.

'General, most people in the south of the country already think that you should be our next president, and recently you have been gathering massive support here in the north as well. What's your secret?'

Sophie cleared her throat, leaned over to the microphone and translated the question into French for the General.

Crêpe-Sombo chuckled. 'I have no secrets,' he said. 'I can only say that people here in the north are very clever. They realise that I love them and that I will lead them strongly.'

Sophie rolled her eyes and translated the General's words into Fulfulde.

'When I am president,' continued the General, 'I will plant trees, dig wells and give every child in Gorom-Gorom a mosquito net.'

Yeah right, thought Sophie, but she translated all the same.

'Your griot is the talk of the town,' said the presenter. 'Could he treat our listeners to another of his superb songs?'

Sophie translated and General Crêpe-Sombo beamed. 'Certainly,' he said. 'Gidaado the Fourth would like to perform a song about Amadou Spinola, my main rival for the job of president.'

Sophie threw a questioning look at Gidaado.

'Amadou Spinola intends to visit Gorom-Gorom today,' continued the General. 'You should all know that Spinola is a vile, bad-mannered toad of a man, and that he would make a terrible president.'

Sophie said nothing.

'Translate,' mouthed General Crêpe-Sombo.

Sophie shook her head and sat back in her chair. Praising Crêpe-Sombo was one thing, but insulting his opponent was quite another. She would not do it.

The General's face darkened and his hand bunched into a fist. '*Translate*,' he hissed.

It was Gidaado who came to the rescue. He grabbed his *hoddu* and started plucking the strings so fast that his fingers became a blur.

'*Salam alaykum!*' he cried. 'Here is a ditty which will make you laugh so hard you will fall off your camels!'

Sophie got up and went through into the presenter's cabin. She looked at the mixer desk, microphones and cassette decks, which were all lit by the sun streaming in through a skylight above Ali Cisse's head. General Crêpe-Sombo stayed in his seat and glared at Sophie through the glass. She had clearly upset him and he was a frightening man when he was upset.

Gidaado swelled up and began to sing:

'Spinola is as spineless as the flatworm in his
    gut
And his chronic halitosis makes the bark fall
    off the trees.
I would like the opportunity to kick him in
    the butt.

May his mattress be infested by a thousand
camel fleas!'

Sophie frowned. Usually Gidaado was so
kind when he talked about other people. How
could he sing such horrible things about a man
he didn't even know? She tried to catch
Gidaado's eye, but he was concentrating too
hard on the fingerboard of his *hoddu*.

'His tummy's so enormous that he's never
seen his feet,
And he's never seen a battle for he's yellow
to the core.
He could do a PhD on how to lie and steal
and cheat.
May he fall into an empty well and bother us
no more.'

'Ouch!' spluttered Ali Cisse, who had been
laughing so hard that his coffee spilled all over
his lap. Crêpe-Sombo leaned back in his chair
and smirked. He did not understand Fulfulde but

he knew what the song was about and he was enjoying it immensely.

'You will find his morals lower than the shadow of a snake,

When God was handing brains out he was last one in the queue.

There are no chairs or promises Spinola cannot break.

If they try to make him president I'll move to Timbuktu.'

Gidaado finished with three staccato taps on the body of his guitar, and then stood up and bowed to his audience. Ali Cisse and General Crêpe-Sombo broke into enthusiastic applause, and Cisse turned the 'reverb' dial until it sounded like a whole football stadium was clapping. The deafening applause made the walls of the studio vibrate.

'That was Gidaado the Fourth,' boomed the presenter, 'official praise singer to Presidential Candidate General Alai Crêpe-Sombo!'

Sophie could not take any more of this. She left the presenter's cabin, flounced past Gidaado and the General without a word, opened the studio door and ran out into the warm early morning breeze. She did not look back. She ran past the Land Rover, the cattle market, the baker's oven and the mosque, and as she ran she gulped back tears. She was sorry that she had ever got involved with this horrible campaign.

She turned down a side street and stopped at the fourth gate along. 'Kok-kok,' she called, opening the gate. It was Madame Maasa's place.

Madame Maasa was sitting on a stool in front of her house, happily prodding half a dozen pancakes in a frying pan. The radio on the ground next to her was now playing a song by the Malian musician Ali Farka Touré.

'*Salam alaykum*,' said Sophie. 'I'd like to cancel today's pancakes, please.'

Madame Maasa looked up at Sophie and her smile vanished.

'Don't worry, Madame Maasa,' called a voice, 'she's only joking!'

Sophie swung round. Gidaado was perched on Chobbal's saddle, peering over the mud-brick wall into Madame Maasa's yard. He must have left the radio station shortly after Sophie and followed her footprints in the sand.

'Gidaado!' Madame Maasa's face lit up. 'I just heard your song on the radio. Brilliant! I loved the bit about the flea-infested mattress.'

'Thank you,' said Gidaado.

'I'm not joking,' said Sophie to Madame Maasa. 'We don't want any more pancakes.'

'Yes, we do, Madame!' called Gidaado. 'Crêpe-Sombo is paying for those *maasa* and he wants another thousand today.'

'Good,' said Madame Maasa. 'I'll carry on, then.'

Sophie knew it was no use arguing. After all, it wasn't her money, it was the General's. She felt small and miserable.

'What's wrong, Sophie?' called Gidaado.

'You are.'

Madame Maasa frowned and muttered, 'That's not very nice.'

Sophie turned on her. 'And saying that Amadou Spinola is as spineless as a flatworm, that *is* very nice, is it?'

Madame Maasa chuckled.

'And wishing he would fall down a well, that's nice too, is it?'

'Didn't you like my song?' said Gidaado.

'I hated your song,' said Sophie. 'It was stupid and spiteful and I wish I had never agreed to come with you.'

'You don't understand,' said Madame Maasa. 'This is an election campaign. You have to say bad things about your opponent.'

'It's part of the game,' said Gidaado.

'Really?' said Sophie. 'Well, it's a game I'm not going to play any more.'

'In that case,' said Madame Maasa, 'why don't you run along home and let me get on with my cooking?'

'You don't get it, do you?' said Sophie. 'Your precious General Crêpe-Sombo is like a carnivorous plant. He may be impressive on the outside but if you get too close to him you die.'

Gidaado stared at her. 'What on earth are you talking about?'

'Crêpe-Sombo wants to start a war.'

'Against who?'

'I don't know. I heard his men plotting in the Land Rover last night. They said he was going to declare war.'

'A war against the sand.'

'No!' cried Sophie. 'A real war!'

'You're as mad as a marsh mongoose,' said Gidaado. 'Go to school.'

'Fine,' said Sophie. 'I was just going.'

Chapter 5

Sophie did not go to school. She knew that if she walked into class this late, Monsieur Lapin would be sure to beat her with his *gurmoohi* cane and she did not want that. Instead she went to the marketplace, bought a handful of peanuts and plonked herself down on the ground in the shade of an acacia tree. A few people passed her by but no one greeted her.

A three-legged pig was snuffling around in a

pile of rubbish nearby. Amongst the Fulani people, pigs were a religious taboo: untouchable, inedible and despised by all.

'I know how you feel, pig,' murmured Sophie as she shelled her peanuts. 'I don't have any friends, either. Gidaado was my only real friend in this town, and now I have nobody. Except my dad, of course, and he's more interested in his *Drosophyllum Brownum*.'

Just then a boy came past holding a long stick with a hoop on the end. Sophie recognised him from school but he was not in her class so she did not know his name. The boy slipped the hoop over the pig's head and walked off, dragging the pig behind him.

'Hey,' called Sophie. 'Why aren't you in school?'

'Because I'm working,' said the boy. 'Why aren't *you* in school?'

'Because I'm sitting here eating peanuts,' said Sophie. 'What are you doing with that pig?'

'Can't have pigs in the marketplace. 'It's unhygienic.'

'That's your job, is it? Pig-removal man.'

'Today it is,' called the boy, and he disappeared out of sight behind the fruit-and-nut stall. Sophie had never heard of a pig removal project in Gorom-Gorom. Whatever would they do next? Send people out to pick up all the plastic carrier bags that littered the ground?

Now Sophie was completely alone. Not even a three-legged pig for company.

'PEOPLE OF GOROM-GOROM!' yelled a town crier on the far side of the marketplace. 'AMADOU SPINOLA WILL SOON BE ARRIVING IN GOROM-GOROM! COME TO THE FOOTBALL PITCH AND HEAR THE LEGENDARY STATESMAN MAKE HIS SPEECH!'

'Or at least go and marvel at the statesman's legendary stomach!' joked one of the stall owners. Sophie sighed. Was there anyone in Gorom-Gorom who *hadn't* listened to the radio show this morning?

Sophie got up, brushed the peanut shells off her trousers and wandered off in the direction of the football pitch. She was a foreigner here, and too young to vote, but that did not stop her being interested. She wanted to see Spinola for herself and hear what he had to say for himself.

When Sophie arrived at the football pitch, rows of metal chairs were being laid out under a marquee. The chairs faced a wooden stage on which stood a lectern and a pot of flowers. Nearby a small generator hummed, connected to an amplifier and a lectern microphone. This was the traditional setup for a political meeting in Africa: a stage, some shade, metal chairs, a microphone and a long, long speech.

People started arriving and sitting down on the chairs to wait for Amadou Spinola. They were laughing amongst themselves as they reminded each other of the gags in Gidaado's song. Sophie sat down near the front and waited.

Half an hour later Spinola's car arrived and four people got out: a driver, a large well-dressed woman who had to be Spinola's wife, a military-looking man who had to be his bodyguard and a neat-looking man with a beard who had to be Amadou Spinola himself. The wife and driver took their seats in the front row and Amadou Spinola stepped up onto the stage and approached the lectern microphone.

A ripple of disappointment ran through the assembled crowd. The presidential candidate was portly but nowhere near as fat as Gidaado's song suggested. Spinola could see his feet quite clearly, thank you very much.

'Ladies and gentlemen of Gorom-Gorom,' he began, 'I find exquisite joy in visiting this desert shore, across whose level swathes of sand the lonely herder treks.'

Sophie found Spinola's voice pleasant and easy to listen to, even if his poetic style was a little over the top.

'In the past,' the speaker continued, 'a chief would never leave home without at least one praise singer to extol his name. But this is not the past and I am not yet chief, so let me introduce myself instead. My name is Professor Amadou Spinola.'

Professor, thought Sophie. So much for being last in the queue when the brains were handed out! She doubted now whether Gidaado's song had even a grain of truth in it.

'If you vote for me,' said Spinola, 'here are some of the things I promise to do for your region. Firstly, vaccinations. On the day I come to power, all of your chickens, cows and old women will receive a free flu jab.'

A murmur of approval rose from the crowd. It was inspired not by Professor Spinola's vaccination plan, but by the arrival of some pretty girls with banana *maasa* on their heads and 'I ♥ Crêpe-Sombo' on their T-shirts. Sylphlike, they began to wander up and down the rows. Heads turned. Eyes ogled. Hands reached out to grope for crêpes.

Only when the pancake plates were empty did Spinola once again become the centre of attention. He had doggedly continued his speech throughout the pancake giveaway and he was now talking about the nationwide problem of corruption.

'Corruption,' said Professor Spinola, 'is a dirty, hairy, pot-bellied monster. Every bribe we pay is a succulent monster-snack which makes the monster grow a little bit bigger. Vote for Spinola, and together we will STARVE that pot-bellied monster. Together we will make that monster shrivel up and—'

CRASH!

The wooden boards on the front of the stage fell forward and the next thing Sophie saw was a herd of pigs rushing out from underneath the stage and careering full-pelt into the audience. Chairs overturned. Pigs squealed. Fists flew. Spinola's wife fainted.

'STAMPEDE!!!' yelled Furki Baa Turki.

Chaos filled the tent. Pigs were bad enough when they were snuffling around in the rubbish dumps on the edge of town, but to have them running amok in this chic marquee was intolerable. Baa Jibi Norme jumped onto his chair and started dispensing karate kicks. Muusa ag Bistro leaped forward and seized a pig's tail in each hand, resulting in a scream that sounded like

53

two hundred scary fairies in agony. Amadou Spinola's wife revived briefly, yelled, 'Get your filthy snout out of my handbag!' and fainted again.

When Sophie looked back on the events of that day, she reflected that it might have turned out all right had Salif dan Bari the snake man not got involved. Salif dan Bari had brought to the rally a sack containing his favourite snake, known to the people of Gorom-Gorom as Mamadou the Malevolent Mamba. He had hoped that after Spinola's speech he would get a chance to do his snake routine and sell some New Salif Extra-Plus Anti-Snakebite Pills.

Salif dan Bari opened the sack and threw it high into the air. 'This will give you pesky pigs something to think about!' he cried. Before the sack even hit the sand, Mamadou the Malevolent Mamba was off, streaking along the ground towards the stage.

As bad luck would have it, Mamadou did not chase away the pigs. Instead he headed straight for Professor Spinola's microphone cable which lay on the ground in thick snake-like coils. Perhaps Mamadou mistook it for a female mamba. He hugged the cable tight and slithered along its entire length from ground to stage to lectern to microphone to Spinola.

The people of Gorom-Gorom knew that Salif dan Bari always removed the poison fangs of his exhibition snakes as a health and safety precaution. Unfortunately, Professor Spinola knew no such thing. 'AAAAARGH,' was the Professor's comment as the mamba's jaws locked around his nose.

Spinola's bodyguard heard the cry, saw the snake and panicked. He put his hand to his belt and drew a pistol.

'Don't shoot!' cried Sophie.

'DON'T SHOOT!!!' cried Furki Baa Turki.

The bodyguard shot. His bullet missed Spinola and it missed the mamba but it hit the microphone, which blew up in a shower of sparks and tiny plastic fragments. The microphone was still connected to the amplifier, and the blast which sounded from it was the loudest noise that Sophie had ever heard in her life. Anyone within twenty miles of Gorom-Gorom that day would have thought the universe was ending.

Although the universe had not ended, Professor Spinola's campaign rally unquestionably had. That one ear-splitting explosion emptied the marquee instantly of all men, women, children, pigs and snakes, and ten minutes later some of them could still be seen running.

The event went down in Saharan history as the loudest and least successful political event ever, and the griots of Timbuktu still mark its anniversary with a special musical performance: *The Ballad of Spinola and the Swine*.

Chapter 6

When Sophie got home she found her father staggering around outside holding one end of his extra-long papaya pole. He was trying to knock a large papaya off its branch way up at the top of the tree, but the pole was heavy and difficult to aim.

'How was school today?' asked Dad, without taking his eye off the papaya.

Something's wrong, thought Sophie. *He never*

asks me that. 'School is always the same,' she replied, which was true enough.

Dad tried again to hook his prize, tottering to and fro like a drunken pole-vaulter. 'I listened to *Start the Day with Ali Cisse*,' he said. 'That dreadful Crêpe-Sombo man was on.'

'Ooo, you almost got it that time,' said Sophie, trying to change the subject.

'There was a girl translating for him,' said Dad. 'She sounded a bit like you.'

Sophie's heart skipped a beat. 'Really?'

'In fact, she sounded *a lot* like you. I thought for a moment that my daughter had gone and got herself mixed up in politics.'

'Try to stand still when you poke it,' advised Sophie.

'Then all of a sudden it sounded like she was refusing to translate,' said Sophie's dad. 'That must have upset the General more than a little, wouldn't you say?'

At last! The sharp end of the pole bit through the stalk, and the luscious fruit began to fall. Mr Brown dropped the pole and stuck his hands out in front of him to catch the falling papaya. He clutched and missed and the ripe fruit exploded on the ground.

'Bad luck,' said Sophie.

Mr Brown bent down and flicked a few of the bigger bits of papaya off his trouser legs. Then he straightened up and turned a stern eye on his daughter.

'Never mess with power-hungry people,' he said.

'Somebody has to,' said Sophie.

'Yes,' said Dad. 'But not you.'

There was a long silence. Sophie picked a morsel of papaya off her cheek and popped it in her mouth. 'Dad,' she said. 'What would we do if there was a war here?'

Mr Brown nodded towards his motorbike which stood in the shade of a *gurmoohi* tree. 'We'd jump on the bike,' he said, 'and we'd ride like bats out of hell all the way to the nearest airport. We'd get on the next plane out of here.'

'Where to?'

'Wherever.'

'Just like that?' asked Sophie. 'Run away and leave everybody?'

Dad looked surprised. 'Yes,' he said. 'But it's not going to happen, is it? This country has not been at war for years.'

'I guess not,' said Sophie. 'What's for lunch?'

'I was hoping to make papaya pancakes.'

Sophie groaned. 'I'll put some rice on,' she said.

As she watched the rice pot bubbling away on the stove, Sophie thought hard. One way or another, this country was heading for a war, and she had seen enough television to know how horrible that would be. There was nothing fun about war, nothing at all. Sophie thought of Salif dan Bari, Belko Sambo, Furki Baa Turki and all the other people she knew in Gorom-Gorom, and again she heard that voice: *They'll vote for him now, but the question is, will they fight for him when he declares war?*

The faraway sound of singing broke in on Sophie's thoughts, a high-pitched quavery song that could only be one person. Gidaado must be in the marketplace practising for tonight's Great Pancake Giveaway: another crowd of happy voters, another thousand banana crêpes, another speech by General Crêpe-Sombo. *The pancakes were my idea*, thought Sophie bitterly, *and now they are being used to smuggle a war-mongering fiend into the President's Palace.* She jabbed the ON button on her dad's radio and turned the volume all the way up to drown out Gidaado's inane singing.

The programme playing on the radio was a news show.

'All over the country, election fever is reaching a climax,' read a breathless female newsreader. 'Tomorrow the nation will vote for its new president. Out of fifteen candidates, the two frontrunners are General Alai Crêpe-Sombo and Professor Amadou Spinola. Analysts believe that the vote in the north of the country will be crucial in deciding who gets into power.'

Oh dear, thought Sophie. If that's true then Crêpe-Sombo is bound to win.

'There were alarming scenes in Gorom-Gorom this morning,' continued the newsreader. 'Professor Spinola's Gorom-Gorom rally ended in chaos when Spinola released a herd of pigs into the audience, in what is thought to have been a publicity stunt gone wrong.'

Sophie could hardly believe her ears. Spinola and his wife had been just as shocked by the arrival of the pigs as she was herself. No, it was clear to Sophie that Someone Else had arranged the pig trick. Sophie had got a clear view of the pigs rushing out from underneath the stage, and one pig in particular had caught her attention: it was thin and grey *and it had had three legs*.

This afternoon I will go to school, thought Sophie, *and I will find that 'pig-removal' boy and I will make him tell me the whole story. If he knows about the pigs, maybe he also knows something about the coming war.*

She found the pig-removal boy during afternoon break. He was playing football with his friends on a patch of sand behind the classrooms.

Sophie went and stood behind him. 'Goalie, huh?' she said. 'Let any in yet?'

'Don't talk to me,' muttered the boy. 'I'm concentrating.'

'Did your class teacher beat you for playing truant this morning?' asked Sophie.

The boy ignored the question.

'Mine did,' said Sophie. 'Hurts, doesn't it?'

The boy nodded slightly.

'I asked somebody in your class to tell me your name,' whispered Sophie. 'Nuuhu, they said.'

Silence.

'Anyway,' whispered Sophie, 'I just wanted to tell you, Nuuhu, I thought you were wonderful today. Did you see Spinola's wife when she saw all those pigs rushing towards her?'

Again, silence.

'Get your filthy snout out of my handbag!' screamed Sophie in a shrill falsetto.

Nuuhu made as if he had not heard, but then he suddenly burst out laughing. He couldn't help himself.

'I've been wondering,' said Sophie, 'how did you make them all rush out at the same time like that? It must have been *really* difficult.'

The boy turned to look at Sophie. He seemed to be in two minds whether to talk to her or not. Sophie gazed back at him with wide innocent eyes.

'It was easy,' said Nuuhu at last. 'I used this.'

He held out a small metal whistle.

Sophie took the whistle and blew on it. No sound came.

'It's a dog whistle,' said Nuuhu. 'Only animals can hear it. I was hiding under the stage with the pigs and I suddenly started blowing it like crazy.'

'You're brilliant!' cried Sophie, clasping her hands in front of her. 'Because of you we're bound to win the election.'

'What do you mean, "we"?'

'You and me and Gidaado and the rest of the General's team.'

'Gidaado!' Nuuhu snorted. 'That buffoon knows nothing. He doesn't even come to the planning meetings.'

'Yes, he does.'

'No, he doesn't,' said Nuuhu, 'and nor do you. Not the secret ones.'

Sophie squealed. 'Ooooh, tell me about the planning meetings. I *love* secrets.'

'No,' said the boy. 'My father would kill me if I told you.'

'Go on,' said Sophie. 'Is there one tonight?'

Just then a football flew past them and the boys on the pitch started jeering. Nuuhu had let in a goal.

'Look what you made me do,' he said angrily. 'Go and spoil someone else's game!'

Funny, thought Sophie as she walked away. *That's exactly what I intend to do.*

'Wait!' cried Nuuhu. 'You didn't give me back my whistle!'

But Sophie was already out of earshot.

Chapter 7

When school finished that day, Nuuhu hung around in the classroom with his friends for hours. They chewed cola nuts and told jokes and took turns drawing djinns and bandits on the blackboard. Every now and then one of them would go to a window and spit out a mouthful of bright red cola nut juice. Sophie knew this because she was hiding just outside under one of the classroom windows and got gobbed on more than once.

At last Nuuhu said goodbye to his friends and left the classroom. Sophie watched him disappear into the gathering dusk and then she went and peered at his footprints in the sand. Nuuhu's trainers left a little Nike tick in the middle of each footprint – his tracks would be easy to follow.

Past the mosque, past the baker's oven, past the clinic, past Miki's Motos, and towards the lake Sophie went, stopping only to buy a bunch of bananas. She followed Nuuhu's footprints in the sand and whenever she spied him in the distance she slowed down again to let him get ahead. If he turned round at any time he must not see that he was being followed.

What was it Nuuhu had said? My father would kill me if I told you. *Who is Nuuhu's father*, wondered Sophie, *and what goes on at those planning meetings?* She hoped that she was going to find out before the night was over.

Nuuhu's footprints led to a house on the edge of the lake. The house had two storeys and it was made of concrete rather than mud bricks. If this was Nuuhu's house, his parents must be rich.

The house was in a large yard surrounded by a twelve-foot high wall. All along the top of the wall bits of broken glass glinted red in the setting sun. If someone were to try climbing up, they would get very badly hurt. Nuuhu's family was certainly well fortified.

Sophie walked to the shore of the lake. The water came right up to the back wall of Nuuhu's yard and lapped gently against the concrete bricks. No back gate, then.

There was, however, a jujube tree. It grew out of the lake behind the house and the fork in its trunk was about level with the security wall. Sophie imagined that somebody sitting in the branches of that tree would have a good view of the house and part of the yard. *I have to get up there*, murmured Sophie.

The jujube tree was not far away, but there was no way of reaching it without wading in the lake. What was it that Dad always said? *Never mess with African lakes, Sophie. One little*

*paddle and your legs will be covered with baby
flatworms. They will cling to your skin and make
tiny holes in it and then wriggle right into your
body. Once they are in, they will make their way
to your liver and suck your blood. A few weeks
later they'll swim on down to your small
intestine and lay hundreds and hundreds of
eggs. You'll get terrible tummyache, my dear,
and be as sick as a dog for weeks. Never mess
with African lakes.*

Sophie turned and walked away from the
water. She didn't want flatworms partying in her
liver or laying eggs in her guts, thank you very
much. Ugh! Even the thought of it made her feel
sick.

But as she walked away, she heard a still
small voice at the back of her mind. *There is a
war coming, Sophie. Only you can stop it.*

Sophie hurried back to the lake, closed her
eyes and put her right foot forward into the
water. The foot sank a few inches into the soft
sludge below. *Don't think of the worms.* She
took another step, feeling the sludge close

around both ankles, and then waded forward until the water was up around her knees. *Don't think of the worms. Don't think of the worms.*

It took Sophie ten steps to reach the base of the jujube tree. She clambered up the trunk and wriggled out onto a branch overlooking Nuuhu's yard.

There was an electric strip light planted upright in the middle of the yard, casting a circle of light on the ground. Nuuhu was there. He was busy dragging armchairs into the circle of light.

'Don't forget the blackboard, son,' called a man's voice from inside the house. Sophie started. It was the same voice that she had heard in the Land Rover – the one who had talked of war.

Sure enough, when the man came out of the house a moment later, Sophie recognised him straight away. He wore an army uniform and a jagged scar led from his left eye down to his chin. *Lieutenant Yameogo!* So it was he who had wrecked Professor Spinola's speech – and he had got his son to do his dirty work for him!

Sophie felt something bite her hand and only then did she notice the column of fire ants marching up and down the branch she was lying on. She grimaced. The last place in the world she wanted to be right now was hanging over Gorom-Gorom lake sharing a branch with an army of fire ants. But she had no choice. She was about to witness the last secret planning meeting of General Crêpe-Sombo's inner circle!

Ten minutes later Sophie heard the squealing of Land Rover brakes and a heavy knock on the front gate. Nuuhu opened the gate and in walked General Crêpe-Sombo himself, followed by his bodyguard Pougini.

'Where are you, Lieutenant Yameogo?' boomed the General, striding towards the house. 'There's only one thing worse than being late, remember?'

'Running away from a battle!' laughed the Lieutenant, coming out of the house. The men shook hands and sat down in the armchairs around the strip light.

There was a long silence and then General Crêpe-Sombo spoke. 'I think we have an uninvited guest in our midst,' he said.

Sophie felt sick. She had been spotted already! What a terrible spy she was.

'Sorry, General,' said the Lieutenant. 'Nuuhu, how many times do I have to tell you? Doing odd jobs for us does *not* make you a member of this committee. Go to your room!'

Nuuhu slunk back to the house and the meeting started. Crêpe-Sombo took a stick of chalk from his pocket and began to sketch on the blackboard what looked like a map of West Africa. Sophie was top of her class in geography and she recognised the shapes of the various countries as the General drew them: Mali, Burkina Faso, Ivory Coast, Niger, Benin, Togo...

The General was talking in a low voice now, as if he were afraid of being overheard. He started marking rivers on the map – long sweeping lines going from country to country. Sophie's eyes widened. *Wait a minute! Those are not rivers – those are arrows. They're troop movements!* She strained to hear what the General was saying, but she could only catch a few phrases: 'Plan our strategy …mobilise an army…march north… hardly any border sentries …'

Sophie wriggled further and further up the branch and received five bites from angry fire ants. But she could still not hear properly, she was simply too far away. And even if every word were crystal clear, what good would it do? Who would believe a ten-year-old girl's claim that the president-to-be was preparing an army to go to war with his neighbouring countries? *What I need is proof*, thought Sophie, and straight away an idea flashed into her mind. It was so crazy it just might work.

Chapter 8

Sophie edged back along the branch, scrambled down the tree, waded to the shore and set off towards the marketplace, sprinting as fast as a scary fairy on steroids. Running in the dark was dangerous and Sophie stumbled frequently, but somehow she arrived at the marketplace without spraining an ankle.

There in the middle of Crêpe Plaza stood Gidaado the Fourth, brandishing his *hoddu* and practising what looked like a tap dance. Chobbal the albino camel was kneeling nearby, watching his master's antics with a bleak gaze.

'Gidaado!' cried Sophie, running to him. She had expected to find him here, but was delighted all the same.

'Sophie,' said Gidaado. 'Do you want to hear my new song?'

'No time,' panted Sophie. 'You have to come with me *right now*.'

'It's a special version of Crêpe-Sombo's family tree, and there's a conga dance that goes with it.'

'Gidaado, listen to me.'

'And get this,' said Gidaado. 'Right after the Pancake Giveaway we're going to get the *entire crowd* doing the dance.'

'Listen to me!'

'Just imagine that, Sophie. Four thousand people doing the Creepy-Crêpe Conga around the edge of the marketpl— OUCH!'

'Come with me,' said Sophie.

'I can't. I'm practising for tonight.'

'Gidaado,' said Sophie. 'You're my only friend. And right now, I need you.'

Chobbal the albino camel was well known for his speed. When he ran at full pelt all you could see was a large white blur and when he passed by it took half an hour for the dust to settle again. He would certainly have won last year's Provincial Camel Race had he not been felled by a sleep dart only yards from the finish. Some said that Chobbal could outrun the harmattan wind, but that claim had never been properly tested.

Small wonder then that it took only eight and a half minutes for Sophie and Gidaado to arrive back at the lake. That included a pit stop at Sophie's house to pick up her cassette player, a roll of Sellotape and her dad's extra-long papaya pole.

Chobbal knelt down and the children slid off his hump.

'You remember what to do?' Sophie whispered.

'I remember,' whispered Gidaado. 'But I promise you, we're wasting our time here. Crêpe-Sombo is a dove. He's the most peace-loving General the army ever had.'

'We'll see about that,' said Sophie, stepping into the water. She waded to the jujube tree and clambered up into the branches. Gidaado passed her the extra long papaya pole and Sophie pulled it up into the tree. Only then did she look over the wall into Lieutenant Yameogo's yard.

The committee meeting was still in progress. General Crêpe-Sombo was pointing at the blackboard and he seemed to be answering questions from the Lieutenant. There was still time for Sophie to get the proof she needed.

Sophie opened her shoulder bag and took out the cassette player and Sellotape. She picked leaves off the branches around her and stuck them onto the machine until it looked like a small shrub.

There was a knock on the gate, and the Lieutenant jumped up to answer it.

'You!' he exclaimed when he saw Gidaado standing there. 'What the *zorki* are you doing here?'

Gidaado's voice carried clearly on the night air. 'Nuuhu told me there was a planning meeting here tonight. Am I late?'

'You are not late, because you are not invited!' bellowed Lieutenant Yameogo. Sophie noticed the General turn the blackboard around so that Gidaado could not see it.

'Not invited?' said Gidaado. 'But I'm the General's praise singer. I'm practically his campaign manager!'

While all eyes were on Gidaado, Sophie lowered one end of the pole down over the wall into the yard, heaving on her end to move it into position.

'This meeting is none of your business,' said the Lieutenant. 'Go back to the marketplace and wait for us there. We will be with you in time for the Pancake Giveaway.'

Perfect. The far end of the papaya pole came to rest in a flowerbed just behind the blackboard.

So far so good. Don't turn around, Crêpe-Sombo. Keep your eyes on Gidaado.

'Talking of the Pancake Giveaway,' said Gidaado, 'here's a little dance I prepared earlier.' He grabbed Lieutenant Yameogo's waist and began to jig from side to side.

> 'Come and do
> the Creepy-Crêpe Conga!
> Fill your face,
> Then come and join the fun!'

Lieutenant Yameogo had no intention of doing the Creepy-Crêpe Conga tonight or any other night. He wheeled round and seized Gidaado's ear in an iron grip.

'Get OUT of here!' yelled the Lieutenant.

'AAAAAAAARGH!!!' cried Gidaado, and at that exact moment Sophie pressed RECORD on her tape recorder and let it go. It slid all the way down the papaya pole and landed in the flowerbed just behind where Crêpe-Sombo was sitting. *Result!* Sophie pulled the papaya pole quickly back into her tree. *Well done, Gidaado*, she thought. He had timed the distraction perfectly and no one had seen the pole.

The Lieutenant threw Gidaado out, slammed the gate and returned to his armchair. The meeting continued. Sophie still could not hear exactly what was being said, but one thing was sure – her tape recorder was hearing every word! For twenty minutes Sophie sat in the tree munching jujube fruit and watching the men in the yard below. Fire ants bit her occasionally but she was so excited she did not notice them.

At seven-thirty the meeting ended. 'Nuuhu!' called Lieutenant Yameogo. 'We're going to the rally.'

'Uh-huh,' said a sulky voice from the house.

The men went out of the gate and Sophie heard the low growl of the Land Rover's engine. The time had come for her to retrieve the evidence. She reached up and felt around for a strong bent twig that she could use as a hook. When she found one, she stuck it into the end of the papaya pole and wound it round with

Sellotape until she was sure it would not break. Then she lowered the pole over the wall.

Gently does it. Sophie gripped the branch tight between her knees and used both hands to direct the papaya pole towards her precious tape recorder.

Sophie hooked the twig underneath the handle of the tape recorder. 'Gotcha,' she murmured. Then she glanced up and saw General Crêpe-Sombo coming in through the gate. He had forgotten his chalk.

A good soldier is able to assess a situation quickly and decide on the proper course of action, and General Crêpe-Sombo was nothing if not a good soldier. A lesser man would have been surprised to see a papaya pole looming out of nowhere with a shrub hanging off the end. A lesser man would have stayed rooted to the spot with his mouth hanging open. Not General Crêpe-Sombo. The moment he clapped eyes on that pole, all the General's military instincts screamed 'SECURITY BREACH' and he bounded forward to intercept it.

Sophie yanked the pole upwards so that it hung in the air just out of the General's reach, her triceps straining to keep it aloft. She was grateful for the twelve-foot high wall which separated her from Crêpe-Sombo, grateful also for the strip light down in the yard which shone in her enemy's eyes and prevented him from seeing her. With an extra heave, she raised the papaya pole up above her head, and jiggled it so that the tape recorder slid down the pole towards her.

Crêpe-Sombo flung out a ham-like fist which smashed the strip light into smithereens, then stood dead still and gazed up at the tree. He took off his shirt, tore it in two, and began to wrap the fabric around his hands. Sophie stared. *I don't believe it. He's going to climb the wall. He's going to come straight for me.*

General Crêpe-Sombo was famous for his ability to get onto the roof of a Land Rover in two bounds without a run-up. But that was nothing compared to the athletic feat that Sophie now witnessed. The General ran flat out towards the wall and then at the last moment he threw his head back and *ran up it*, grabbing the glass-topped parapet with his bandaged hands and pulling himself up until he was standing on top of the wall. He launched himself out across the water, seized the end of Sophie's branch and swung himself up so that he was sitting on top of it.

'*Bonsoir*, Sophie Brown,' said General Crêpe-Sombo.

Chapter 9

Sophie had no desire to chat with General Crêpe-Sombo, or to watch any more athletics. She grabbed her tape recorder, dropped the papaya pole into the water below and slithered down the tree trunk.

The General's weight proved too much for the jujube branch he was sitting on. It snapped, and he dropped into the water below. Sophie waded towards the shore as fast as she could and

General Crêpe-Sombo came after her, ploughing through the sludge with long powerful strides.

As Sophie reached the edge of the lake, a pair of arms reached out for her and yanked her up onto a white camel hump.

'Good evening,' said Gidaado. 'Fancy a ride?'

'Yes,' said Sophie. 'Quick!'

Crêpe-Sombo was not far behind. He clambered up onto the bank, boots squelching, breathing heavily through his nose.

'HOOOSH-BARAKAAAA!!!' cried Gidaado and they were off. The General pursued them for a mile or two but even the fastest soldier in West Africa was no match for Chobbal the albino camel.

'I'LL HUNT YOU DOWN, SOPHIE BROWN!' yelled General Crêpe-Sombo, shaking his fist in the moonlight. 'EVEN IF YOU PAINT YOURSELF GREEN AND MOVE TO GREENLAND, I'LL FIND YOU!'

*

When they were sure they had lost General Crêpe-Sombo, Gidaado and Sophie rode northwards into the desert. Gidaado had a den in the hollow of a baobab tree about two hours' ride from Gorom-Gorom. It was the perfect place to hide and discuss their next move.

'*Zorki*,' said Gidaado, when they were safely inside the baobab den. 'That was a close call.'

Sophie nodded. 'You should have seen General Crêpe-Sombo running up that wall, Gidaado. I'll never forget it as long as I live.'

'Which won't be very long if the General gets his way.'

'Or if the flatworms get their way,' said Sophie. 'I keep wondering if they've reached my liver yet.'

'Don't worry about it,' said Gidaado. 'There's good medicine for flatworms. Swallow four big de-worming tablets tomorrow and you'll be as fit as a *hoddu*.'

'Are you sure?'

87

'Totally. I had flatworms last year and look at me now. Anyway, stopping General Crêpe-Nutter is well worth the irritation of a few worms, don't you think?'

'It's funny,' said Sophie, 'I seem to remember *someone* saying that he's the most peace-loving General the army has ever had.'

'Yes,' said Gidaado. 'That was you who said that.'

'Wasn't.'

'Was.'

'Wasn't.'

'Was.'

'Wasn't.'

A match flared in the darkness and Gidaado lit a paraffin lamp. Sophie had been in this den once before and it was just as she remembered it: the walls of the chamber were smooth and they were lined with shelves. On one shelf there were bowls, on another was fruit, on another lay Gidaado's spare *hoddu*.

'Let's hear your cassette, then,' said Gidaado.

Sophie took the tape recorder out of her shoulder bag and pressed REWIND. She was looking forward to finding out exactly what had gone on at General Crêpe-Sombo's secret planning meeting.

'Which way's Greenland?' said Gidaado.

'North.'

'Further than Yengerento?'

'Yes.'

The tape finished rewinding and Sophie pressed PLAY. They heard the distant cries of Gidaado being thrown out of the meeting, and then silence. The silence was broken by the voice of General Crêpe-Sombo.

'Does your son tell our secrets to *every* person he meets, or just the insane ones?'

'Sorry, General. I will discipline Nuuhu severely.'

'Do that. Now, back to business. You asked me a question, Lieutenant?'

'Do you really think our army is strong enough to invade Mali?' said Lieutenant Yameogo. 'Their army is twice the size of ours.'

The men were talking in French, so Sophie stopped the cassette and translated into Fulfulde for Gidaado.

'You're joking!' cried Gidaado. 'Did he really say that?'

'I'm afraid so,' said Sophie, pressing PLAY again.

'I have the solution,' said the voice of General Crêpe-Sombo. 'I will close down every school in the country and draft all the pupils into the army. Just imagine it: the largest, fittest fighting force in the whole of Africa. They will cross the border into Mali *here*' – the sound of chalk on blackboard – 'take over the gold mines *here* and *here*' – more chalk – 'and then build fortresses all along the Dogon cliffs – *here* and *here* and *here* and *here* and *here* and—'

'Hold on,' said the Lieutenant. 'What makes you think that people will support such a war?'

'We'll blow up the Ministry of Agriculture in Ouagadougou and we'll say Mali did it.'

Sophie had heard enough. She leaned over and jabbed the STOP button.

'You've gone green,' said Gidaado. 'Are you OK?'

'I need air,' said Sophie. She scrambled up the rope ladder and out into the branches of the baobab tree. Gazing over the level sands, it did not seem possible that this peaceful region was so close to disaster. *I will close down every school in the country and draft all the pupils into the army. Just imagine it.*

Gidaado joined her in the fork of the tree. 'Are you all right?' he asked.

'Of course not,' said Sophie. 'That man is going to close the schools and make us all join the army. Except for his own daughter, of course, who is safe in Paris. While we're dodging bullets on the Dogon cliffs, pretty little Marie Crêpe-Sombo will be nibbling croissants on the Champs-Élysées.'

'It's not her fault,' said Gidaado hotly. 'Besides, the war might not be as bad as you think. They'll probably give us guns.'

Sophie turned on him. 'Yes, let's hope so,' she said. 'Then we can wave our guns about and wear sand camouflage and eat sugary biscuits out of pretty foil packets. It'll be brilliant right up until the moment the planes of Mali's airforce arrive. When the bombs start falling on our heads, you can tell me whether or not war is as bad as I think!' She put her head in her hands and burst into tears.

'Everything happens for a purpose,' said Gidaado.

'Well, this isn't going to happen at all,' said Sophie, wiping away her tears. 'We're going to stop it. We're going to make sure that people don't vote for Crêpe-Sombo.'

'Count me out,' said Gidaado. 'I'm his praise singer. I refuse to plot against the person who pays my wages.'

Sophie snorted. 'You think he'll be paying you any more wages after you helped me escape tonight?'

'I don't care. It's the principle of the thing.'

Sophie stared at her griot friend and for once in her life she was completely lost for words. There followed a long silence.

'OK, fine,' said Gidaado at last. 'You're right and I'm wrong. What's the plan?'

'We hide here till morning,' said Sophie, 'and then we pay a little visit to Gorom Radio.'

Chapter 10

'No, no, no, no, no,' said Ali Cisse, the presenter at Gorom Radio. 'Absolutely not. No.'

'But it's important,' said Sophie. 'This cassette *proves* what kind of a man General Crêpe-Sombo really is.'

It was five to seven in the morning and Ali Cisse was having a cup of coffee in the presenter's cabin and getting ready for his *Start the Day with Ali Cisse* show. Sophie and

Gidaado had been waiting for him when he arrived at the station at sunrise, and they were taking it in turns to plead with him.

'If you had come to me yesterday morning,' said Cisse, 'I might have been able to help you. But today is Election Day – all campaigning is officially over.'

'We are not campaigning,' said Sophie. 'We are exposing the truth. At least let us play you a sample, and then you can decide for yourself.'

Ali Cisse took a sip of coffee. 'I've already decided,' he said, 'but you and your friend seem to be hard of hearing.'

Sophie went and crouched next to the presenter's swivel chair. They were so close their noses were almost touching. 'Do you have children, Mr Cisse?'

'Eleven of them.'

'How would you feel if they had to join the army?'

'The discipline might do them good,' said Cisse. 'It might stop them turning out like *you*.' He chuckled and took a swig of coffee.

'Fine,' said Sophie, and she walked out, slamming the door behind her.

Gidaado was waiting for her in the main studio. 'Any luck?'

'What do you think?' said Sophie.

They went out into the morning sunshine and closed the door behind them. Sophie sat down on the step and put her head on her hands.

'One ... two ... three ... ' she counted.

'Come on, let's go,' said Gidaado, climbing up into Chobbal's saddle.

'Four ... five ... six ... '

'What are you doing?'

'Counting to twenty-five,' said Sophie.

'Why?'

'That's how long it takes.'

'Eh?'

Sophie grinned and held up a tiny sachet containing yellow powder. '*Drosophyllum Brownum*,' she said, 'discovered by Mr Simeon Brown two years ago and crushed into a powder by Miss Sophie Brown two hours ago.'

Gidaado goggled at her. 'What does it do?'

'I'll show you.'

The children crept back into the studio and peered through the window into the presenter's cabin. Ali Cisse was slumped forward with his head on the mixing desk, snoring loudly.

'You slipped some of that powder into his drink?' said Gidaado.

Sophie nodded. 'Coffee has such a strong taste, it masks pretty much anything. Come and help me move him.'

'Move him?' Gidaado looked puzzled. 'Why?'

'Because we have a show to put on, and we can't have him snoring in the background!'

Ali Cisse's swivel chair was on wheels so it was easy for Sophie and Gidaado to get him out of his cabin, through the studio and all the way out of the building. Sophie removed the presenter's keys from his pocket, and then they went back into the studio and locked themselves in.

Sophie took her tape recorder out of her shoulder bag, placed it on the table in the main studio, and set it to RADIO mode. 'What frequency is Gorom Radio?' she asked.

'98.8 FM,' said Gidaado.

'I'll say this for you griots,' said Sophie. 'You have brilliant memories. Tune the radio to 98.8 and wave at me when you hear my voice.'

Sophie carried a chair into the presenter's cabin and closed the door behind her. She sat down and frowned at the various pieces of audio equipment in front of her. Microphone. Cassette deck. Mixer. Transmitter. *This had better work*, thought Sophie. *Otherwise all the children in this country are toast*.

The clock on the wall showed seven o'clock exactly. It was time for *Start the Day with Ali Cisse*. Sophie pulled the microphone towards her as she had seen Ali Cisse do, and she turned on the red ON AIR lamp. She flicked a switch on the mixer and it hummed into life. The green indicator light on the transmitter started winking at her in a friendly way.

'SALAAAAM ALAAAAAAAAAYKUM, GOROM-GOROM!' cried Sophie. 'You are listening to *Start the Day WITHOUT Ali Cisse* and this is your host Lala Lacrosse!'

Sophie peered through her window into the main studio and saw Gidaado frowning and shaking his head. It was not working. Sophie flicked the mixer off and on and fiddled with some of the slider controls. 'Hello?' she said in a small voice. 'One ... two ... three ... testing.'

Gidaado put his ear right up close to the radio and shook his head sadly. It was three minutes past seven. Any longer and people would start arriving at the station asking why their favourite wake-up show was not on this morning. Besides, Sophie was not sure how long the effect of the Phyllis Powder lasted – for all she knew Ali Cisse would be waking up any minute and wondering what he was doing outside and where his microphone had got to.

The microphone! Of course! Sophie looked closely at the stem of her presenter's microphone. There was an OFF/ON switch and right now it was in the OFF position. Sophie flicked it to ON and started her introduction again:

'SALAAAAAAAAM ALAAAAAYKUM, GOROM-GOROM!' cried Sophie. 'You are listening to Gorom Radio, 98.8 FM, and this is your host Françoise Frigo!'

Gidaado leapt off his seat and punched the air. Sophie took that as a good sign and carried on talking.

'Welcome to this special Election Day edition of *Start the Day without Ali Cisse*, and what a treat we have in store for you today. Get ready to hear the innermost thoughts of your very own "Man with a Plan": General Alai Crêpe-Sombo!'

Sophie turned the 'reverb' dial to max as she had seen Ali Cisse doing, and clapped her hands in front of the microphone. Gidaado grinned and gave her a thumbs-up sign. 'Go, girl!' he mouthed at her through the glass.

'The interview you are about to hear was recorded in French,' said Sophie. 'If you don't understand French, grab someone who can translate it for you.'

Sophie looked down at the mixing table in front of her; she slid the microphone control to

QUIET and the cassette deck control to LOUD. Then she inserted her cassette and pressed PLAY. Lieutenant Yameogo's voice came through the studio speakers.

'Do you really think our army is strong enough to invade Mali? Their army is twice the size of ours.'

'I have the solution. I will close down every school in the country and draft all the pupils into the army. Just imagine it: the largest, fittest fighting force in the whole of Africa...'

Sophie leant back in her chair and put her hands behind her head. She imagined the agitated scenes in homes all across Gorom-Gorom as people listened to the General's words.

'...We'll blow up the Ministry of Agriculture in Ouagadougou and we'll say Mali did it. On the whole people are very stupid, you know. If a building explodes and the president says so-and-so did it, people won't question it.'

Gidaado poked his head round the door of

the presenter's cabin. 'It's Crêpe-Sombo,' he said.

'Of course it is,' said Sophie. 'We listened to the whole thing last night, remember?'

'No, I mean, there's someone knocking on the studio door right now – and it's Crêpe-Sombo.'

Chapter 11

The children tiptoed into the studio. Sure enough, an iron fist was pounding on the front door, causing it to shake on its hinges.

'I know you're in there!' roared General Crêpe-Sombo. 'Don't make me break this door down.'

'What do you want?' said Sophie in a quavering voice.

'I've been listening to the radio,' replied the

General, 'and I would like a word with Françoise Frigo. Or should I say SOPHIE BROWN?'

The pounding on the front door redoubled in force, wrenching one of its three hinges out of the wall.

'Don't let him in!' cried Gidaado, trembling from head to foot.

'IS THAT YOU, GRIOT?' yelled General Crêpe-Sombo. 'DO YOU KNOW WHAT WE DO TO TRAITORS IN THE ARMY?'

Sophie and Gidaado looked around them wildly. There was nothing to hand with which to defend themselves and there was no back door to the studio. The General gave the door a vicious kick and another hinge popped off.

'Quick!' cried Sophie. 'The presenter's cabin!'

The children rushed into the cabin and Sophie locked the door behind them. They peered through the glass into the main studio and saw to their horror that the last hinge was beginning to tear away from the wall. Maybe Dad was right all along, thought Sophie. *Never mess with power-hungry people.*

The recorded voice of General Crêpe-Sombo continued to boom from the studio speakers: 'Some say that war is bad. They could not be more wrong! War is beautiful. War is a theatre in which we test the strength of our resolve.'

Sophie reached for the mixer controls. She slid the cassette control to QUIET and pulled the microphone towards her. 'This radio station is under attack by General Crêpe-Sombo,' she said into the microphone. 'Please, somebody help us.'

At that moment the last hinge gave way and the front door fell forward into the studio with an almighty crash. General Crêpe-Sombo bounded over the threshold and looked around. When he saw the two children cowering in the presenter's cabin, he grinned and began to prowl towards the soundproof window like a panther preparing to pounce.

'Gidaado,' said Sophie. 'The skylight!'

Of course! The presenter's cabin was lit by a

small skylight, just big enough for a child to wriggle through. Gidaado jumped onto the mixing table and reached for the skylight. He wrenched it open and pulled himself up onto the roof.

The General let loose a flying kick and the soundproof glass shattered into a million tiny pieces.

'Sophie!' yelled Gidaado. 'Take my hand!'

The General leaped through the shattered window and made a grab for Sophie's legs as they disappeared through the skylight. He got her left sandal but that was all.

'He's coming after us!' cried Gidaado.

Gidaado need not have worried. The General's chest was wide and the skylight was narrow. He wriggled halfway through and got stuck.

'POUGINI!!!' roared General Crêpe-Sombo.

The children crawled to the edge of the roof and looked down. Pougini and Lieutenant Yameogo were leaning against the Land Rover, waiting for their boss to come out. When Pougini heard his name being shouted he dashed into the studio, leaving the Lieutenant on guard.

'Where on earth has Chobbal got to?' whispered Sophie.

Gidaado pointed. The albino camel had wandered off to a nearby acacia tree and was facing away from the radio station, completely engrossed in munching thorns. '*Zorki*,' said Gidaado. 'There's no way I can call Chobbal without the Lieutenant hearing.'

Sophie delved into her pocket and brought out the dog whistle. 'Nuuhu showed me this yesterday,' she whispered. 'I must have forgotten to give it back.'

'Forgotten?' said Gidaado.

Sophie grinned. 'I'm very forgetful,' she said. 'Besides, who knows when a dog whistle might come in handy?'

Sophie blew hard on the whistle and Chobbal looked round in surprise. When he saw Gidaado waving at him, the albino camel left the tree and loped towards his master, still chomping a thorn branch between his tough gums.

At that moment Pougini burst out of the radio station. 'They're on the roof!' he yelled. 'Stop them!'

The Lieutenant looked up. He saw the children crouching on the edge of the roof, he saw them jump down onto the saddle of a very white camel and he saw the camel run off as fast as the harmattan wind.

'After them!' Lieutenant Yameogo and Pougini jumped into the Land Rover and sped off in pursuit.

Chobbal's hooves pounded hard against the ground and Sophie bounced up and down in the saddle like a cowgirl in a rodeo. Saharan air blasted in her face like an enormous hairdryer.

'Hey, Gidaado, which would you say is faster?' yelled Sophie. 'A camel or a Land Rover?'

'It depends on the camel,' yelled Gidaado, 'and also on the Land Rover.'

'All right, then, which is faster: Chobbal the albino camel or a Land Rover Discovery 3?'

'The Land Rover Discovery 3. Easily.'

'Right. Thought so.'

Sure enough, the Land Rover was gaining on them. Sophie did not dare imagine what would happen when their pursuers caught them up. She knew for sure that they were desperate men. Their plans had been spoiled and all they had left was the satisfaction of revenge.

Then Sophie noticed that the Land Rover was not the only vehicle behind them. Six motor-cycles were careering along behind the Land Rover, and as they got closer, Sophie recognised the markings – Gorom-Gorom police bikes! Someone at the police station must have been listening to the radio and heard Sophie's appeal for help!

'Hey, Gidaado, which is faster?' yelled Sophie. 'A Land Rover Discovery 3 or a Yamaha 250 motorbike?'

'The Land Rover!' yelled Gidaado.

'Oh dear,' said Sophie.

They were galloping north in the open desert. Fulani shepherds and their sheep stopped open-mouthed to watch the convoy pass: a white blur of a camel, a black blur of a Land Rover and six terrier-like motorbikes with their engines screaming.

The van was right on Chobbal's tail now. Sophie turned in the saddle and was shocked to see cruel smiles on the faces of their pursuers. It was clear that they were not going to show any mercy, even with six police bikes behind them.

'Gidaado!' screamed Sophie. 'They're going to run us down!'

'It's been nice knowing you!' yelled Gidaado.

'You too!' yelled Sophie.

The front bumper of the Land Rover touched Chobbal's tail and he snorted in fright. Poor Chobbal! The albino camel was going to come to a sticky end and there was nothing Sophie could do about it. Unless ...

'Gidaado!' yelled Sophie. 'Is there any of that acacia branch left in Chobbal's mouth?'

Gidaado craned his neck to look. 'Yes,' he shouted. 'He's only eaten half of it. It's not easy to eat while you're sprinting!'

'Give it here!' shouted Sophie.

Gidaado took the thorn branch from Chobbal's mouth, and passed it to her. Sophie turned round so that she was facing backwards in the saddle. She leaned down as far as she could. She would only have one chance to get this right...

There! Sophie dropped the acacia branch just in front of one of the Land Rover's wheels. The tread of the tyre came down right on top of a long, strong thorn and POP! The tyre blew out. Pougini lost control of the van. It veered off to the left and immediately started losing speed. The children carried on galloping and Sophie saw the Land Rover skid to a halt in a drift of sand, where it was immediately surrounded by police bikes.

'What happened?' shouted Gidaado. 'What did you do?'

'I threw away Chobbal's breakfast,' said Sophie.

'He'll never forgive you!' laughed Gidaado.

Chapter 12

The shadows of day were lengthening and fading and the sun gradually turned a deep crimson. Sophie and Gidaado were sitting on wicker chairs outside Sophie's house, listening to the radio. A newsreader was gabbling in French about the astonishing events of the day.

'The mysterious recording of General Alai Crêpe-Sombo was first played on Gorom Radio, but before long it was being relayed by radio stations all over the country. By the time voting started in the Presidential Elections, everybody had heard about the General's plan to attack Mali with an army of children. Voting is now closed and unofficial reports suggest a landslide victory for Professor Amadou Spinola. Meanwhile, General Crêpe-Sombo and Gorom-Gorom army chief Lieutenant Yameogo have been arrested by police on charges of vandalism and attempted murder...'

Sophie turned off the radio and smiled at Gidaado.

'So what's the news?' said Gidaado, who did not understand French.

'It looks like they're going to make Amadou Spinola President,' said Sophie.

'HOORAY!' cried Gidaado.

'You're happy about that, are you?' said Sophie.

'Of course.'

'In spite of his spinelessness?'

'Yes.'

'In spite of his halitosis?'

'Yes.'

'In spite of his PhD in how to lie and steal and cheat?'

'I might have exaggerated those things.'

'So you won't be moving to Timbuktu?'

'Not just yet.'

'Good,' said Sophie. 'Happy Election Day.'

'Happy Election Day,' said Gidaado.

Read other stories about Sophie and Gidaado:

SOPHIE AND THE ALBINO CAMEL

Then Sophie saw it. At the end of the row was a camel which was white from head to hump to hooves. There were lots of normal brownish camels but then this beautiful white one. She looked at its face. Usually camels look like they are smirking, but this one didn't. It looked serious, maybe even a little sad. It turned its big brown eyes towards Sophie and gazed at her from under half-closed eyelids. Its eyelashes were very long.

'*Salam alaykum*,' said a voice behind her.

Sophie spun round and saw a small boy. He was wearing baggy trousers with patches on both knees, and a yellow shirt with sleeves far too long for him. He was leaning on a long staff and grinning at her.

'*Alaykum asalam*,' said Sophie.

'Ugly, isn't he?' said the boy.

'No, I think he's beautiful,' said Sophie. 'I've never seen a white camel before.'

'And he's never seen a white girl before,' said the boy. The boy's head was shaved completely bald and his front teeth stuck out a little. He looked friendly.

'What is his name?' asked Sophie.

'Chobbal,' said the boy. Chobbal was a kind of African food – a spicy rice pudding which Sophie did not like very much.

'I've never seen you at Gorom-Gorom school,' said Sophie.

'I don't go. I am a griot.'

Sophie had heard of griots but never met one. Griots were professional storytellers so they knew thousands of stories, riddles and songs. They were experts in African history, too – a good griot could remember the names and adventures of all the warriors and chiefs of his region during the past five hundred years. Whenever there was an important party, a baby's naming ceremony for example, the host of the party would hire a griot to come and sing for the guests. On these occasions the griot's songs were usually about how brave and wise and good-looking the host's ancestors all were.

'Do you want to hear my *tarik*?' said the boy.

'Okay,' said Sophie, not understanding the word.

The boy raised his arms and took a deep breath in, until his whole body seemed to swell up. Then he started to sing in a high-pitched wail:

> '*Hail, my name is Gidaado the Fourth*
> *Gidaado the son of Alu*
> *Alu son of Hamadou*
> *Hamadou son of Yero*
> *Yero son of Tijani*
> *Tijani son of—*'

'Okay,' said Sophie. 'That's enough I think.'

> ' *– Haroun son of Gidaado the Third*
> *Gidaado the Third son of Salif*
> *Salif son of Ali*
> *Ali son of Gorko Bobo—*'

'Stop,' said Sophie.

'Gorko Bobo son of Adama
Adama son of Hussein the Tall
Hussein the Tall son of Gid – OUCH!'

'Sorry,' said Sophie, letting go of Gidaado the Fourth's ear.

Gidaado rubbed his ear and scowled. 'What's your name?' he said.

'Sophie,' said Sophie.

'Nice to meet you,' said Gidaado. 'I think.'

'Likewise,' said Sophie.

There was a sound of snoring from behind them. The animal park attendant had fallen asleep again.

'I should be heading back to my village,' said Gidaado.

'Okay,' said Sophie.

'Tell me something, Sofa,' said Gidaado, his face slowly breaking into a grin. 'Would you like a ride on Chobbal?'

Sophie looked at the beautiful white camel and then at Gidaado. Say 'no' to strangers, her dad had always told her. But hadn't he also told her to try and make some friends?

'All right,' said Sophie.